Dave Saunders trained at Brighton Art College.
He worked as a primary school teacher for many years
and is now a full-time illustrator of children's books.
Together with his wife, Julie Saunders, he has created
several young picture books for Frances Lincoln, including
The Ducks' Tale, The Ducks' Winter Tale, and *The Big Storm,* and
is the illustrator of *Down by the Pond* by Margrit Cruickshank.

Dave and Julie live in Malvern Link, Worcestershire.

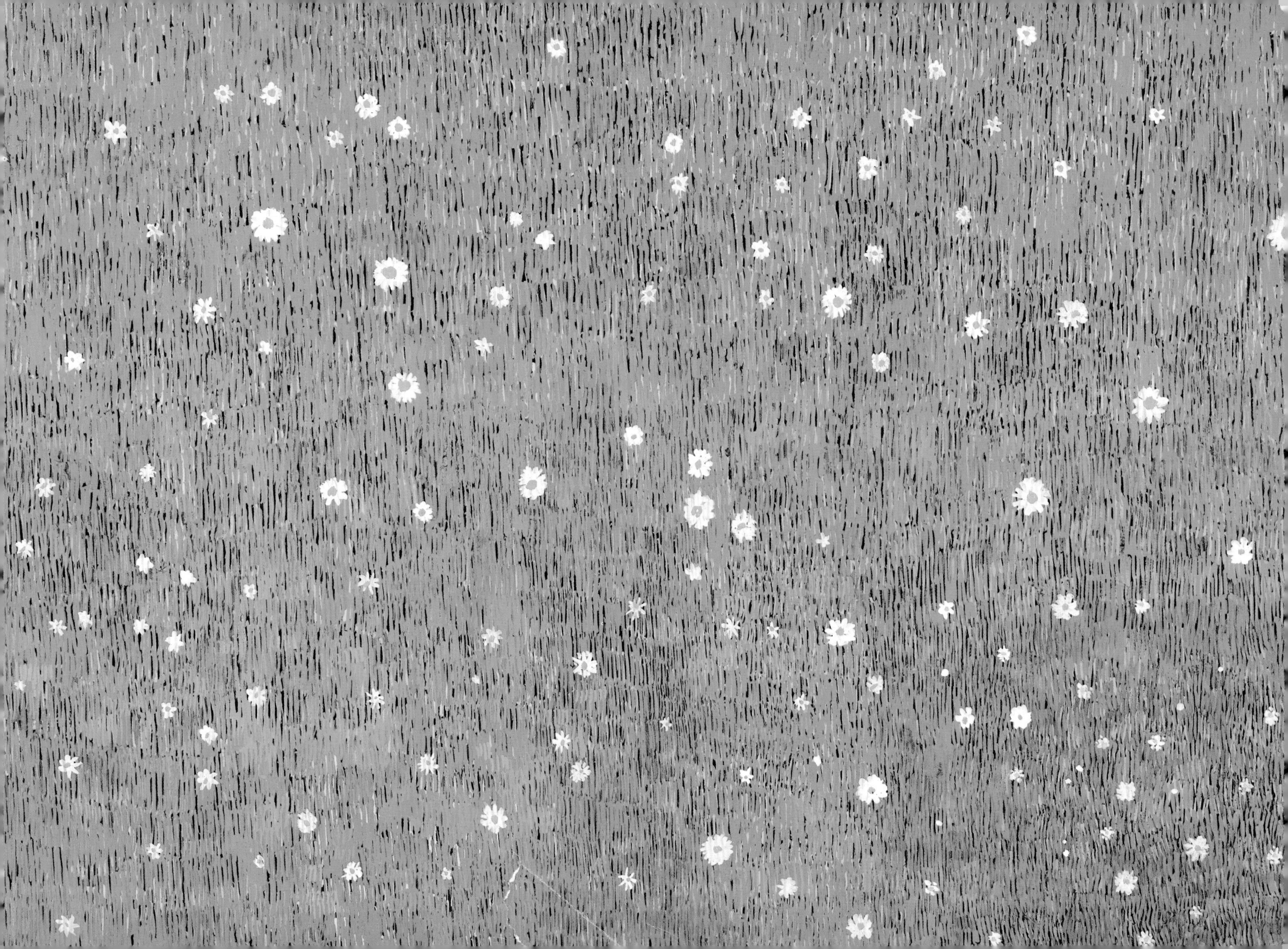

For Penny and David

First published in Great Britain in 1993 by
Frances Lincoln Limited, 4 Torriano Mews
Torriano Avenue, London NW5 2RZ

British Library Cataloguing in Publication Data
available on request

ISBN 0-7112-0760-7 hardback
ISBN 0-7112-0761-5 paperback

Printed in Hong Kong

3 5 7 9 8 6 4 2

THE BRAVE HARE

Dave and Julie Saunders

FR ES LINCOLN

Hare sat up in the daisy field.

"How hungry I am!" he said. "Tonight I will go to the big, big cabbage field for a feast of cabbages. I shall call in to see my friends at the farm on the way."

Hare leapt through the fields.
The sun was low in the sky as he raced down
to the farm.

First he came to the kitchen door where Cat was feeding.

"Cat," said Hare, "I am going to the big, big cabbage field to feast tonight."

"You can't do that!" said Cat. "An old man guards that field – you mustn't go there."

But Hare only twitched his nose.

Hare and Cat came into the orchard where the Hens were feeding.

Cat said, "Hare is going to the big, big cabbage field to feast tonight."

"Oh, no, no, no!" clucked the Hens. "A fierce farmer guards that field – you mustn't go there."

But Hare only twitched his ears.

Hare, Cat and the Hens saw Goat feeding in the field.

Cat said, "Hare is going to the big, big cabbage field to feast tonight."

"Oh, no!" bleated Goat. "An enormous giant guards that field – you mustn't go there."

But Hare only twitched his paws.

The sun was setting when Hare, Cat, the Hens and Goat found Goose feeding in the long grass by the barn.

Cat said, "Hare is going to the big, big cabbage field to feast tonight."

"Oh, no!" honked Goose. "A terrible creature guards that field – you mustn't go there."

But Hare only twitched his tail.

It was beginning to grow dark and Pig had just finished feeding at his trough in the yard. He looked up surprised. "Why are you all here?"

Cat said, "Hare is going to the big, big cabbage field to feast tonight."

"Oh, no!" grunted Pig. "A great flapping monster guards that field – you mustn't go there."

But Hare only twitched his whiskers.

"Well, I am going," laughed Hare, "for I am the brave Hare! Old men, fierce farmers, enormous giants, terrible creatures and great flapping monsters don't bother me. Follow, if you dare!"

The animals looked anxiously at each other. "Shall we go?"

"We must," said Pig, "or Hare will think we're frightened stick-in-the-muds. We *must* show we are as brave as he."

Hare led the way, and behind came Goose, Pig, the Hens, Goat and Cat – through the hedge and over the dark land.

At last they reached the edge of the big, big cabbage field.

"Stay here!" said Hare. "I am the brave Hare, so I will go forward and look."

The other animals huddled together. What was going to happen?

Hare bounded through the cabbages to
the feet of . . .

a scarecrow!

They all crept forward
to take a look whilst Hare
feasted on the crispest,
freshest, greenest cabbages
he had ever tasted . . .
. . . crunch, crunch, crunch.

MORE PICTURE BOOKS IN PAPERBACK FROM FRANCES LINCOLN

THE DUCKS' TALE
Dave and Julie Saunders

Two curious ducks spot a furry snake by the riverbank, and find they are in for a big surprise!

"Top choice for the younger children - indeed, it could hardly be bettered." Naomi Lewis, *The Observer*

Suitable for National Curriculum English - Reading, Key Stage 1
Scottish Guidelines English Language - Reading, Levels A and B

ISBN 0-7112-0608-2   £4.99

THE BIG STORM
Dave and Julie Saunders

Dark clouds are gathering over the wood. "Hide and shelter!" cry the animals
one by one, running into their holes and burrows. As the storm breaks,
the Squirrels find an unlikely hiding place and, when the rain stops,
a surprise treasure-trove as well!

Suitable for National Curriculum English - Reading, Key Stage 1
Scottish Guidelines English Language - Reading, Level A; Environmental Studies, Level A

ISBN 0-7112-0865-4   £4.99

DOWN BY THE POND
Margrit Cruickshank and Dave Saunders

A red fox crept across the yard, his black-tipped tail was twitching hard in the farmyard
down by the pond . . . In this twist in the tail romping rhyme, a peaceful farmyard
erupts into riotus hullabaloo.

Suitable for National Curriculum English - Reading, Key Stage 1
Scottish Guidelines English Language - Reading, Levels A and B

ISBN 0-7112-0978-2   £4.99

Frances Lincoln titles are available from all good bookshops.
Prices are correct at time of publication, but may be subject to change.